A DOG'S TALE

—LIFE LESSONS FOR A YOUNG PUP—

For Emma, Elsie and Emile, and thanks to Linas – M.R.

To Walter and Dorothy – T.R.

First published in 2019 by Scholastic Children's Books

Euston House, 24 Eversholt Street, London NW1 1DB

A division of Scholastic Ltd

www.scholastic.co.uk

London • New York • Toronto • Sydney • Auckland • Mexico City • New Delhi • Hong Kong

Text copyright © 2019 Michael Rosen • Illustrations copyright © 2019 Tony Ross

ISBN 978 1407 18857 7

All rights reserved

Printed in China

10 9 8 7 6 5 4 3 2 1

The moral rights of Michael Rosen and Tony Ross have been asserted.

Papers used by Scholastic Children's Books are made from wood grown in sustainable forests.

A DOG'S TALE

—LIFE LESSONS FOR A YOUNG PUP—

MICHAEL ROSEN • TONY ROSS

SCHOLASTIC

Hey, what's with the frown? Let's go for a walk.
You know what they say: it's helpful to talk.

I've been round the block
and on trains once or twice;
there's no harm in hearing an old dog's advice.

Tomorrow it starts! You'll be on your way.
But don't you be worried: *you will be OK.*

An adventure begins!

It's your very first bite
     of an epic life story
          that YOU get to write.

So tail up, get ready! Be wide-open-hearted!
The world is there waiting for you to get started.

Fill up on hope, throw away fears,
keep those paws clean and prick up your ears.

What happens tomorrow will all be **brand-new**,
with great things to sniff! And great stuff to chew!

With Frisbees to catch,

and rabbits to chase,

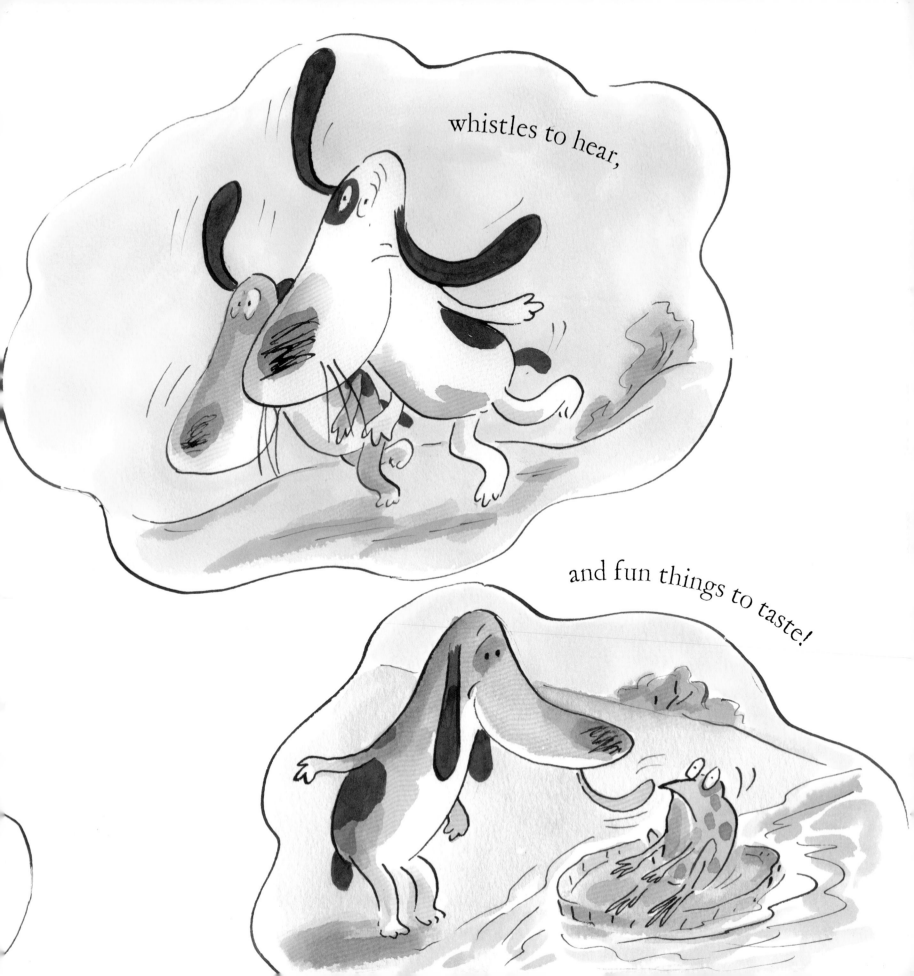

You'll run down big roads!

Through the woods!

To the beach!

You will not **believe** all the hilltops to reach!

Wherever you travel
you can make a mark!

Make yourself heard –
use your biggest, best

bark!

Now don't get me wrong: I'm not going to claim
that everything's easy, that life's a big game.

While digging a hole,
with your nose in the ground...

a thing might pop out!
And knock you right down.

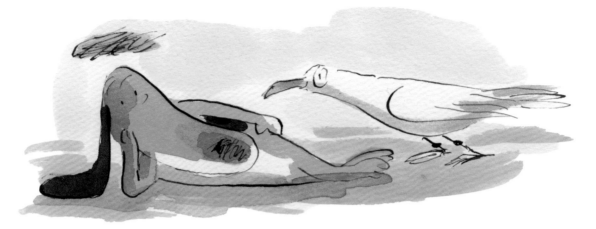

Now, whether you're old or just a young pup,

what matters the most is how you get up.

And sometimes it rains! You might have to take it.
Your fur will get wet –

don't worry: just shake it.

Someone you love might leave you behind,
and a feeling of sadness won't leave your mind.

It's good to know then,
when you're left on your own,
that this doesn't mean
that you're all alone.

So when you are lost
and can't find the track,

a friend will be there

to point the way back.

Slowly but surely,
you'll be on the mend.
You may soon discover:

now YOU
are the friend.

You'll find there are others who will look to YOU.
To give THEM the answers for what they should do.

The world is a bowl that we should all share.

We're happiest when we know it's been fair.

My advice for you, dear, before I go for a doze,
is this: keep it simple.
Just follow your nose.

At the end of the day, when sunset is fading,
come on back home...

I'll be here waiting.